for a.a., for dreaming with me

Produced by the Department of Publications
The Museum of Modern Art, New York

Christopher Hudson, Publisher
Chul R. Kim, Associate Publisher
David Frankel, Editorial Director
Marc Sapir, Production Director

Commissioned by Éditions du Centre Pompidou
on the occasion of the exhibition *Magritte: La Trahison des
images*, September 21, 2016–January 23, 2017

Edited by Chul R. Kim, Emily Hall, and Cerise Fontaine
Designed by Amanda Washburn
Production by Hannah Kim
Printed and bound by Taeshin Inpack, Ltd.
This book has been printed using soy ink, which is less toxic
and more biodegradable than conventional inks. It also
reduces volatile organic compound (VOC) and hazardous
air pollution (HAP) emissions.

With thanks to Marie-Sandrine Cadudal, Claire de Cointet,
Cari Frisch, Charly Herscovici, Elizabeth Margulies,
Nicolas Roche, Anne Umland, and Wendy Woon.

This book is typeset in Futura and Samantha.
The paper is 150 gsm woodfree.

Library of Congress Control Number: 2016941476
ISBN: 978-1-63345-016-5

Published in English by The Museum of Modern Art
11 West 53 Street
New York, New York 10019
www.moma.org

Published in French by Éditions du Centre Pompidou
75191 Paris Cedex 4, France
www.centrepompidou.fr

English edition distributed in the United States and Canada
by Abrams Books for Young Readers, an imprint of
ABRAMS, New York

English edition published outside the United States and
Canada by Thames & Hudson Ltd.

Printed in Korea

Photography Credits

klaas verplancke

Magritte's Apple

the museum of modern art,
new york

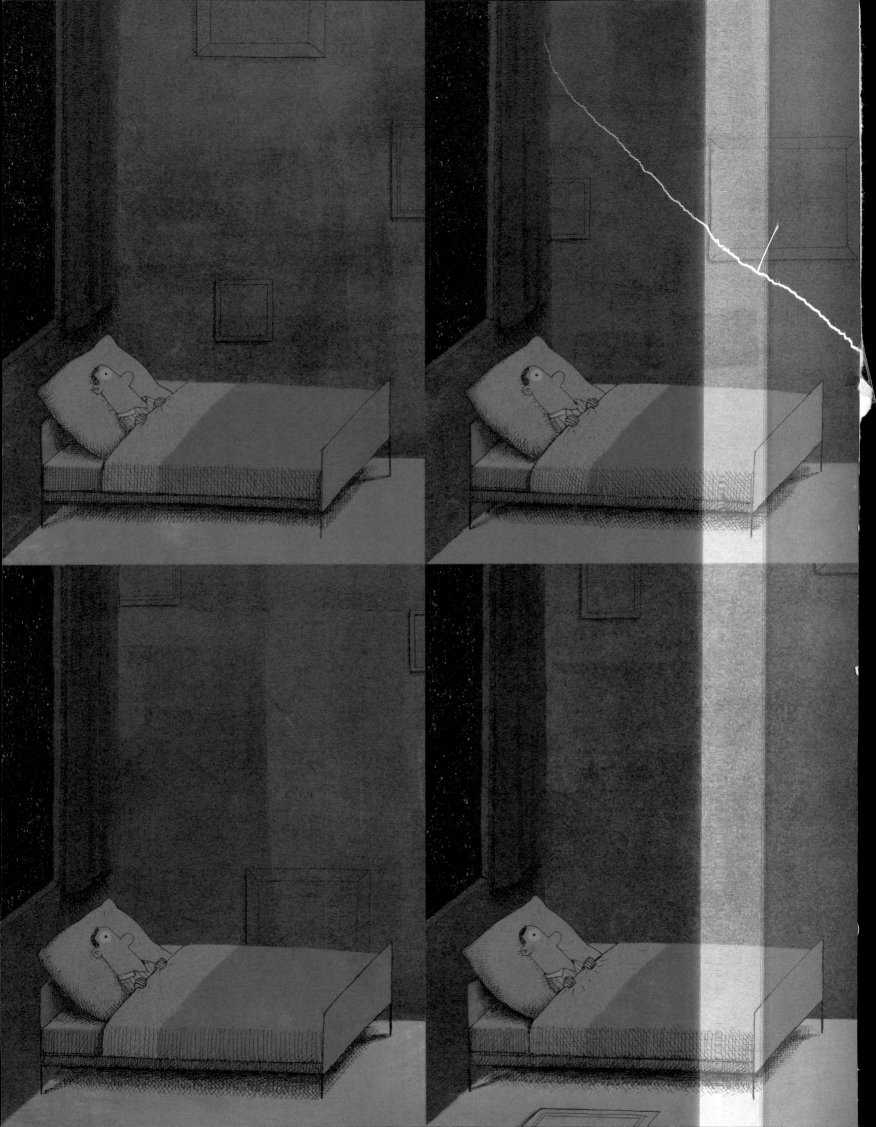

René was a painter,
but René couldn't paint.
He knew how, but he didn't know what.

Because René couldn't paint,
he couldn't sleep.

When he got out of bed in the morning,
his canvas was still empty.

His canvas was empty,
but his head was full.

Full of ideas about objects and words.

But where to start?

He dreamed about
being a painter…

...a painter of apples.

He dreamed about being a painter of hats.

A painter of applehats…

...a painter of butterleaves, branchpipes, and spectacleggs.

An egg became a bird when he painted it.

Shoes turned into feet.

the chair

the mirror

the giant

night

the wind

tree

He was a painter
of words and things,
and sometimes
his words
described other
things.

sunlight

nothing

He was a painter of paintings.

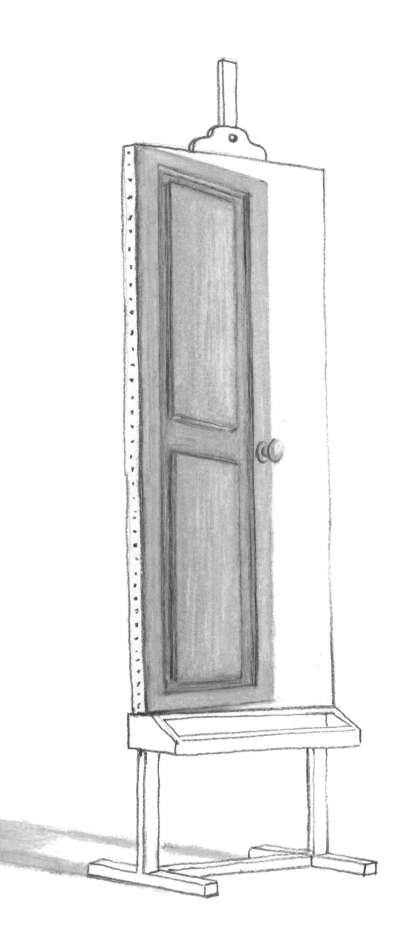

He liked to enter them
and exit them.

knock, knock

He painted the impossible
so that it was possible.
He painted the extraordinary
so that it was ordinary.

An apple can lead you to
some very interesting places.

Can *you* find objects in this book from these paintings by René Magritte?

L'Empire des lumières II (*The Empire of Light II*). 1950
Oil on canvas, 31 x 39 in. (78.8 x 99.1 cm)
The Museum of Modern Art, New York. Gift of
D. and J. de Menil

Le Portrait (*The Portrait*). Brussels, 1935
Oil on canvas, 28⅞ x 19⅞ in. (73.3 x 50.2 cm)
The Museum of Modern Art, New York. Gift of
Kay Sage Tanguy

La Clairvoyance (*Clairvoyance*). Brussels, 1936
Oil on canvas, 21¼ x 25⁹⁄₁₆ in. (54 x 65 cm)
Private Collection

Le Modèle rouge (*The Red Model*). 1935
Oil on canvas, mounted on panel,
22 x 18⅛ in. (56 x 46 cm)
Centre Pompidou, Musée national d'art
moderne, Paris

Les Amants (*The Lovers*). Paris, 1928
Oil on canvas, 21⅜ x 28⅞ in. (54 x 73.4 cm)
The Museum of Modern Art, New York. Gift of
Richard S. Zeisler

Le Palais de rideaux (III) (*The Palace of Curtains [III]*). Paris, 1928–29
Oil on canvas, 32 x 45⅞ in. (81.2 x 116.4 cm)
The Museum of Modern Art, New York. The Sidney and Harriet Janis Collection

René Magritte (1898–1967)

René Magritte and *Le Barbare* (*The Barbarian*). London, 1938. Photographer unknown
Gelatin silver print, 7 3/8 x 9 7/8 in. (18.8 x 25 cm)
The Baltimore Museum of Art. Purchase with exchange funds from
the Edward Joseph Gallagher III Memorial Collection; and partial
gift of George H. Dalsheimer, Baltimore (BMA.1988.440)

René Magritte was born on November 21, 1898, in Lessines, Belgium. He began to paint when he was twelve years old, and in 1914 he moved to Brussels to study at the Royal Fine Art Academy. After trying out a few different styles of painting, he began to paint the everyday objects that populate much of his work.

Magritte was an important part of the Surrealist movement, in which artists and writers used both simple and wildly imaginative imagery to create works that were unexpected, confusing, and sometimes troubling. Magritte combined the real world with fantasy, challenging viewers to guess the meanings of his paintings: "Everything we see," he said, "hides something else." The movement began in Paris in the early 1920s, with writers and then artists who experimented with the relationship between words and meanings. The Surrealists were deeply affected by the absurd horrors of World War I. Rather than relying on logic, since the world was no longer logical, they made art from dreams, imagination, and games.